just add GLITTER

ANGELA DITERLIZZI &
SAMANTHA COTTERILL

BEACH LANE BOOKS *New York London Toronto Sydney New Delhi*

Bored, ignored, or feeling down?
Need some fancy in your town?
Want some shine upon your crown?

Just add glitter!

Try a speck,
a fleck, a sprinkle.

See how things
begin to twinkle.

A little here,
a little there.

Glitter, glitter anywhere!

Is your bedroom such a bore?
How 'bout sparkle on your door?
Could your art use something more?

Just add glitter!

A dash, a dusting,
or a touch.

It's so small but
does so much.

A little here,
a little there.

Glitter, glitter anywhere!

Are your walls asking for glitz?
Looking for more flashy bits?
Time for puttin' on the ritz?

Just add glitter!

A pinch, a cupful,
or a mound.

Glimmer, shimmer
by the pound!

A little here,
a little there.

Glitter,

glitter

everywhere!

Have you made your whole world gleam?
Do you love this glistening dream?
Then grab a ton, have fun, and scream . . .

"Add MORE
glitter!"

Uh-oh. STOP.
We've got enough.
We're *lost* in all this sparkly stuff.

I thought we needed all this bling,
but it's too much of a good thing.

The glitter made it hard to see,
what sparkles most . . .

is you and me.